VAMPIRE PETER

For Rebecca – B.M.
For Viago, my favorite vampire – H.P.

American edition published in 2021 by Andersen Press USA,
an imprint of Andersen Press Ltd.
www.andersenpressusa.com

First published in Great Britain in 2020 by Andersen Press Ltd.,
20 Vauxhall Bridge Road, London SW1V 2SA

Text copyright © Ben Manley 2020
Illustrations copyright © Hannah Peck 2020
Romanian translation by Ileana Hunter

Distributed in the United States and Canada by
Lerner Publishing Group, Inc.
241 First Avenue North
Minneapolis, MN 55401 USA

For reading levels and more information, look up this title at www.lernerbooks.com.

Library of Congress Cataloging-in-Publication Data Available
ISBN 978-1-72843-892-4

1–TOPPAN–5/1/21

VAMPIRE PETER

BEN MANLEY   HANNAH PECK

Andersen Press USA

Peter was the baddest boy in school.
He appeared one day from a faraway land.

And everything he did was strange.

He wore strange clothes.
He ate strange food.

He liked strange things.

And his family was even stranger.

† "Shall I destroy her, your Majesty?"
†† "No, Orlok. She's my friend."

Because Peter didn't fit in,
he didn't have many friends.
And he was always in trouble . . .

For showing off in gym class.

For scaring Mr. Renfield.

For fighting on the playground.

For not telling the truth.

But it wasn't Peter.

It was me.

I opened the cage to stroke Jonathan.
And I forgot to close the door.

I was worried I'd get into trouble, so I said nothing.
And I let Peter take the blame.

After all, he was the
baddest boy in school.

But when I thought about it,
I knew that wasn't true.

He made me laugh
when I was sad.

He played with me when I
was on my own.

He stood up for me when I was in trouble.

Peter was my friend.

It was my turn to stand up for him.
I had to do the right thing.

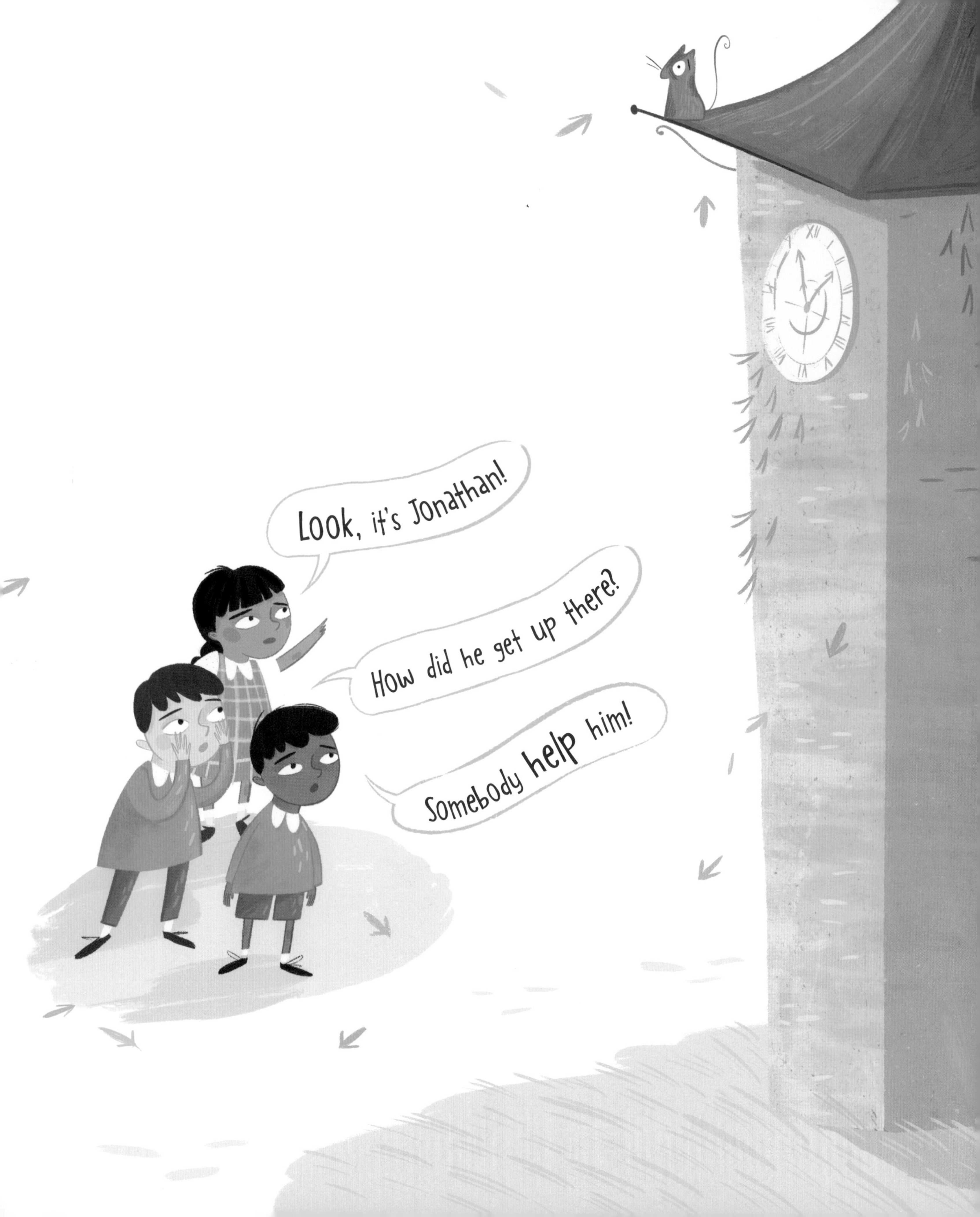
Look, it's Jonathan!
How did he get up there?
Somebody **help** him!

I did a terrible thing.
And I thought I would never be forgiven.
But I was wrong.

Everyone said Peter was the
baddest boy in school.
And maybe sometimes he is.

But most of the time,

Peter is the best.